I0764604

THE REVENGE OF

RIKKI-TIKKI-TAVI CONFRONTS A NEW ENEMY

By...... Peter J. Hylak

THE REVENGE OF ZIRAK

RIKKI-TIKKI-TAVI CONFRONTS A NEW ENEMY

A short story by...... Peter J. Hylak

12/23/05

Revised 03/01/08

Edited by... Bridget G. Hylak

TO MY GRANDKIDS WHO REMIND ME

OF THE WONDER OF YOUTH.

Acknowledgement

This story was written with the help and encouragement of many friends and family members. I would like to thank my daughter and editor Bridget Hylak for her superior insight, suggestions and editing, all of which polished a rough story into professional writing. I also owe thanks to Oksana for an early review that highlighted several storyline weaknesses, and to Enza for her counsel in the beginning. Last and most important, for this story and for the story of my life, I thank my wife Maria who encourages me in all my pursuits with unending praise.

Rudyard Kipling's exciting tale of the mongoose *Rikki-tikki-tavi* may not have entirely ended with the author's final pen stroke.

With a cup of tea in hand on a chilly England night, Kipling might easily have imagined this intriguing sequel that reflects the same brilliance and suspense as Kipling's other great works. *The Revenge of Zirak* picks up from Kipling's original garden ending in which decades ago, *Rikki-tikki-tavi* left many readers hungering for more.

Mr. Kipling grippingly relayed Rikki-tikki's struggles and triumphant battle with the cobras Nag and Nagaina. Desperate to protect his human family, Rikki-tikki demonstrated limitless valor in order to save the family's lives and secure for them a peaceful future. Rikki's final act of completion was to destroy the entire clutch of cobra eggs that Nag and Nagaina had left behind.

Or so he thought...

Rikki-tikki did destroy the cobra eggs nestled together in the well-hidden burrow. What he did not know, and what only his worst nightmare would reveal, was that the female cobra Nagaina had taken great pride in one particular egg of her clutch. Nagaina's motherly instincts assured her that this egg, far larger and more beautiful than the others, would somehow dominate, protect and secure the heritage of all the rest. So sure was she of this preordained destiny that she carefully and lovingly separated this egg from the others, hiding it under a leaf in the melon patch. The large melon leaves, naturally efficient at absorbing and retaining heat, would become the perfect incubator that would best contribute to the egg's development.

This egg, which would alone survive Rikki-tikki's rampage in defense of his family, was the prenatal home of Rikki's soon-to-be sworn enemy, Zirak.

Nagaina visited, admired and turned her special egg daily to regulate the heat. She lovingly caressed it with gentle hisses of motherly cobra pride. Due to its size and her own instincts, she knew it was a male.

Shortly thereafter, her instincts proved correct when a tiny male cobra

– strong, alert and beautiful – emerged from the egg. Nagaina almost smothered her newborn son with kisses of joy. "You are Zirak, the firstborn offspring of myself and the great cobra Nag! You will lead the destiny of our family!"

Nagaina then gentled her enthusiasm and sweetly hissed, "Rest under this melon and gather your strength, my son. There are many worms here for you to eat. It will be several days before your siblings hatch, and your father and I have some humans to deal with until that time comes."

"What do you mean?" asked Zirak in a tiny yet amazingly confident cobra voice. "Maybe I can help, dear Mother."

Nagaina's heart burst with pride at the thought of her newborn son so ready to help her. "Surely this son of Nag will make the finest of warriors," she thought. Despite his eagerness, her motherly wisdom was firmly in charge. "No, son. Not yet. You rest here, and gather your strength; your father and I can solve this problem on our own." With a farewell hug and hiss to little Zirak, she left to find Nag. Zirak admired his mother's great beauty and strength as he watched her slither confidently away from the melon patch.

Little did either one know that this would be their first and last embrace. Zirak, soon to be orphaned by Rikki-Tikki, would shortly become his mortal enemy.

Those of us familiar with Kipling's classic will recall that the great turmoil which ensued in *Rikki-tikki-tavi* was precipitated by a simple transfer of a British lieutenant and his family to a new post. The lieutenant with his wife and son Teddy were assigned living quarters in a nearby vacant house and garden.

The house had a peaceful atmosphere with exotic views and numerous birds and seemed perfect for the lieutenant's family. Unfortunately, they were unaware that it also was home to two large cobras, Nag and Nagaina. The cobras enjoyed this abandoned area and had claimed it as their home for several years prior to the family's arrival. They had just started a family and were determined to protect their clutch of eggs and to evict the human trespassers with their sharp fangs. Shortly after the lieutenant and his family moved into the abandoned house, the terrifying attacks began.

The first emergency occurred early one morning. Entering at night through the outdoor sluice pipe, Nag tried to ambush the humans by hiding in the bathroom and delivering a fatal bite. Though he thought he was well-hidden, he was soon discovered and destroyed by the ever-vigilant Rikki-tikki. Rikki-tikki skillfully fought a fierce battle with Nag and finally bit him sharply in the neck. Holding him tightly while Nag thrashed about wildly, Rikki observed out of the corner of his eye as Nag knocked over several trays and a soap dish before gasping for his last breath. Once all traces of life ceased pulsating through Nag's slithery body, Rikki-tikki dropped him to the ground in a heap.

Nagaina soon learned of her husband's death, and in a fit of rage, she planned to attack the family. Unaware of her impending plan, Rikki-tikki was busy patrolling and searching the garden when he discovered a burrow containing Nagaina's almost-hatched clutch of cobra eggs.

Rikki immediately recognized the urgency of the situation. The baby cobras inside the eggs were already using their birth tooth to open the shells and would emerge momentarily.

Without hesitation, Rikki began quickly yet carefully destroying the eggs, all the while remaining conscious of the fact that young cobras are born with well-developed fangs, poison and the total capacity to kill. These baby cobras were already active and about to leave their shells. Rikki-tikki carefully bit through the shell and the back of each cobra's neck simultaneously to prevent any chance of an accidental reflex bite from their fangs. One by one, he was eliminating the baby cobras when suddenly, he was interrupted by a blood-curdling scream.

The tailorbird's wife frantically shouted that Nagaina, the female cobra, had cornered Teddy and his family in the house. Intending to exact her revenge for the death of her husband, Nagaina slithered closer toward the young master Teddy and his parents. Furious and embittered at being left a widow, she prepared to bite each human in turn. Now, alerted by the tailorbird, Rikki-tikki had a another crisis to deal with.

Rikki-tikki was distressed and enraged at the same time. How could he prevent Nagaina from striking and injecting her deadly poison into the family? Just how many life-threatening emergencies could he handle in the space of one day?

Quickly Rikki-tikki formulated a plan. He took one of the remaining live eggs from the clutch and carried it in his mouth while running furiously to the cottage where Nagaina was poised within striking distance of Teddy. He placed the egg on the ground and confronted Nagaina.

Nagaina recognized the egg instantly; she was concerned and distracted just long enough for the family to escape into the safety of the cottage. Faced with no better alternative, Nagaina swooped up her egg and dashed for the safety of her burrow. Fearlessly, Rikki-tikki chased her and then carefully followed her inside.

Facing Nagaina in the darkness of her burrow was a dangerous move on Rikki's part. Sharp fangs versus tooth and claw, the battle outcome was far from certain. Wily Nagaina had years of experience over the young mongoose, and odds would favor her as the final winner; but Rikki-Tikki's love and passion to protect his family provided him additional strength and stamina.

As luck would have it, Rikki-tikki gained an additional advantage when the already grief-stricken widow Nagaina realized with horror that most of her eggs had been broken and the young cobras inside were dead. Her attention was divided and she became preoccupied with saving her remaining eggs.

In that instant Rikki was able to subdue her. With a lightning move too quick for a human eye to follow, he clamped his jaws on Nagaina's neck. He instantly knew he had hit the mark. With his mind flashing back to his recent triumph over Nag, Rikki-tikki held steady, eyes staring straight ahead, as he now felt Nagaina's body squirm and thrash about. With each whip of her tale, Nagaina's energy diminished until finally, Rikki could feel her lifeless neck in his jaws. After firmly clamping down through her flesh one last time, Rikki dropped Nagaina's lifeless body to the ground next to her clutch of broken eggs. It was over.

Once again, Rikki-tikki had rescued his human family. Against overwhelming odds he had accomplished the triple task of eliminating Nagaina, her husband and then finally the remnants still alive from the clutch of cobra eggs. Exhausted, Rikki-tikki crawled up the path, returned to the cottage and nuzzled into Teddy's arms. All the eggs were destroyed, or so Rikki thought, each baby cobra bitten through the back of the neck. His human family was now safe. Not a trace of cobra remained… except for the single, hidden egg which had already hatched and released Rikki's formidable future foe…Zirak!

Rikki-tikki did destroy the hidden nest of almost-hatched eggs. However, in his haste to return to his family, and exhaustion from a long day of battle, Rikki-tikki had not adequately investigated the surrounding area. Besides, what could be left? His battle fatigue convinced him that no further steps were necessary since the entire cobra family had been destroyed. However, had Rikki taken a moment to sniff, smell and search the garden, he would have found the single surviving young cobra, hidden in the melon patch by Nagaina... Zirak, who would soon become Rikki's formidable and most embittered enemy.

Thus, Kipling's tale of *Rikki-tikki-tavi* concludes, and the saga of Zirak begins...

ZIRAK'S INFANCY

At that point Zirak was only several days old and would have been an easy enemy to defeat. Unfortunately, Rikki was oblivious to Zirak's newborn existence. This baby cobra, orphaned because of Rikki-tikki, would live and grow in size and hatred until his eventual face-off with Rikki-tikki many molting seasons later.

Zirak heard the noise and commotion as soon as the tailorbird sounded the alarm about Nagaina's attack. His instincts warned him to stay in hiding, under the melon leaves, until all the commotion and fighting had stopped. When he heard Rikki-tikki call to Teddy and return to the cottage, he felt it was at last safe to explore.

Zirak came out from hiding and slithered slowly to examine the burrow. What a grim sight greeted him! His mother, brothers and sisters were all dead, gruesomely dispatched by the jaws of Rikki-tikki-tavi.

Rikki-tikki had delivered each of Zirak's siblings a killing bite to the back of the neck, right through the shell. Slowly and deliberately, Zirak studied this scene of carnage, gradually reaching an astounding conclusion for a newborn cobra: his mother and siblings had all been bitten through the back of their necks.

The back of his neck, Zirak concluded, was vulnerable and needed to be protected in battle. The back of his neck would be the primary target in any encounter with the mongoose Rikki-tikki-tavi. When he fought Rikki-tikki-tavi – and in his young heart, he had already vowed to do so – he would be prepared. He would swoop and sway and always remember to protect his neck. Indeed, his superior intelligence guaranteed that he would develop strategy and battle skills that would unpleasantly surprise Rikki-tikki-tavi, the so-called "hero" that had rendered him homeless and an orphan.

Zirak hardly had time to grieve when the coppersmith bird's sharp trill joyfully proclaimed that the hero Rikki-tikki had rid the garden of all danger by killing Nagaina, her offspring, as well as the formidable father cobra Nag! Zirak coiled and flew into a blind rage. At least he had hoped his father had been spared, and together the two would seek their just revenge.

Zirak's head was reeling. For a moment he considered rushing to the cottage to avenge his family. He knew he already had enough venom to inflict a deadly bite! He could kill them all if he had a chance! Yet, an instinctive caution told him that he was too weak and too young to battle Rikki-tikki. Reason prevailed over anger, and rather than act rashly, Zirak began to plan his escape.

Before departing the garden, Zirak circled his dead siblings one last time, recording all the details of the scene with his ominous, wide, obsidian-colored eyes. Broken shells and bodies were strewn all over the burrow. Flies had already begun to gather and feed on the remains.

Deep puncture wounds were oozing blood at the back of his mother's neck, as she stared at him from empty eyes which would never again take in the beauty of their garden, their cottage, their home. Her fixed-open jaw would never again whisper, "I love you, my son" which had caressed his prenatal sensibilities. Never again would her sweet hiss tell him how beautiful he looked and how proud she was of his great size. Zirak's heart was in agony and felt as if it would burst within him; only his lack of tear ducts prevented him from weeping uncontrollably. In a state of cold fury, he laid his head next that of his lifeless mother, and swore to return one day to avenge his family's brutal death and take back his rightful legacy.

THE FLIGHT OF ZIRAK

Zirak paused to reflect for a moment. "Where can I hide?" Danger loomed everywhere in the garden, and Rikki-tikki patrolled the area regularly. Besides Rikki, the coppersmith bird would be only too willing to sound an alert. Indeed, all of the animals in the garden — the rabbit, lizard, frog and birds — were elated to see it free of snakes and would certainly sound an alarm instantly if they saw Zirak.

Fortunately, Zirak's survival instincts were finely-tuned. Eons of natural selection had taken his parent's gene pool and combined it propitiously to produce a superior cobra. His natural intuition and intelligence were far greater than any other cobra ever born, as were his speed and physical proportions. From his primeval ancestors he had inherited great size, agility and crafty intelligence, all traits vital for a successful escape. His mother's instincts had been correct: he was far superior to any other newborn.

He scurried out of the burrow through heavy brush back to the melon patch. His movements were slow and deliberate. He kept his head low to avoid being seen and took cover anywhere he could find it. He had just wiggled close to a melon when a Ralij Pheasant flew into the garden looking for a quick meal.

This bird could stamp him to death with its calloused feet and he would be helpless since he could not hope to puncture the tough feet with his fangs at their present size. He wiggled into the underside of a melon as far as he could, until only part of his head and eyes were barely visible. The bird strutted boldly as it searched for lizards, worms or any insect it could catch. He watched it carefully and could not help but admire its fine plumage. This bird had a scarlet red face with a comb of black feathers sticking out like spikes several inches from the top of its head. His entire body was like a shiny, feathered, black tuxedo except for a splash of white on its backside. He came closer to Zirak's hiding place, while Zirak practically stopped breathing to avoid being heard or seen.

Suddenly, a small lizard dashed from hiding, and the pheasant followed in hot pursuit. The bird skillfully snatched up the lizard with its beak and held it tightly for several seconds. It then quickly flew back to its nest where its young were waiting anxiously for dinner.

With the crisis averted, Zirak looked around carefully and continued moving until he reached a footpath at the end of the melon patch. As soon as his belly slithered onto this open trail, he quickly sensed danger. Too many people traveled on this path, and he could be exposed momentarily.

Zirak needed to search for a safer escape route. He spotted a small creek, and in an instant he wiggled through the dense brush and into the water. His instincts relayed a sense of relief, and he felt that he was now safe from attack by humans or mongooses! However, while this creek did remove the chance of physical attack, the route was not hazard-free. The humans used this creek for their garbage and waste disposal, and Zirak now found himself immersed in flowing sewage.

Everywhere Zirak looked there was some type of human waste or trash. Broken jars, rusted iron hinges, spoiled food, a broken wooden chair and even a cracked glass kerosene lamp full of oil contaminated the water. Zirak had to swim around and avoid these discarded items.

The small creek, once vibrant and alive with many aquatic plants, frogs, insects, blue butterflies and beautiful creatures, was now littered with their remains, barren, polluted and destroyed by human waste. Foul smells, debris and dead fish assaulted his delicate senses as he swam for hours in the unpleasant stench. "How could one species cause so much destruction?" he thought.

Finally, the creek turned near an open area where the humans dumped bulky trash. He was able to crawl onto a sandbar near a path leading to a clearing. Once free from the current, he wiggled to the garbage-cluttered clearing and collapsed, exhausted. Ever-wary of danger, he crawled into a large gallon bottle to rest. Once inside he found several juicy worms which he ate greedily. After his exhausting flight and first solid meal, he fell into a deep sleep and remained there for most of the day and night, dreaming of his mother.

When Zirak awoke, he carefully explored his surroundings. He surveyed possible escape routes and danger areas where an unknown enemy might attempt to take him by surprise. Sometimes he would return to the creek where the constant pile-up of debris and trash continually disgusted him. None of the beautiful birds or animals he observed in the garden seemed to live here. Off in the distance his superior vision allowed him to see birds flying, but they were no where near the garbage dump he was forced to call home. His instincts were sharp, and he sensed his own vulnerability; he knew that many creatures could eat or destroy him at his present size. After all, he was a mere fifteen inches long, a tasty morsel for a host of predators. So he decided to stay where he was for a while, near the safety of the bottle, in order to think, grow, and get stronger.

Several weeks passed uneventfully as Zirak ate all the plush worms and meaty insects he could find. Small lizards and toads were also now on his menu. He rapidly gained strength and grew quickly both in body and intellect. At the same time, his heart was burning with hatred and resolve. He meditated frequently on his catastrophic birth, when he left the warmth of his shell, embraced his mother, and only days later was thrust into the chilling reality of a world in which he was already an orphan.

Zirak chewed slowly on his first memories: the gut-wrenching reality of the brutal deaths of his mother, father and siblings. He contemplated various types of revenge. Most of his imagined scenarios of vengeance involved him ambushing Rikki-tikki in the garden whereupon he would paralyze him with a fatal bite and slowly swallow him whole. His vengeful fantasies helped him to pass the time in the dismal surroundings. He was all alone, without a mother, without family, without a home.

Six weeks later Zirak had grown to almost two feet in length. He had outgrown the bottle and moved into a large, cracked, abandoned earthenware jar. The jar was almost six feet tall and had been used to store rainwater for drinking. Now lying on its side, this clay jar was like a small cave for Zirak to live and hide in safely.

One sunny afternoon Zirak began his daily hunt. A large lizard was perched on a pile of rocks soaking up the warm sun. He would make a fine meal! Zirak slowly slithered around the rocks to come up from behind where the lizard could not see him approach. He focused all his concentration on the lizard that was unaware of the impending danger.

Suddenly, Zirak was greeted with an unpleasant surprise. A large rat, hiding underneath a pile of trash, sprang toward him with jaws snapping at his tail. The hunter had become the hunted! Zirak coiled in fury to protect his tail. He had made such a stupid mistake! How could he have let his guard down and allowed this trash-dwelling creature to surprise him?

"What have we here?" the rat asked. “Could this be a tasty treat for my lunch?"

Zirak lunged to reach the safety of his jar; once in the jar he could protect the entrance with his sharp fangs. His idea was quickly foiled, as the rat jumped and barred his way. A feint to the left and then to the right, and still the rat was covering Zirak’s escape and preventing him from reaching his jar. To the front or side was open ground were the rat could catch him easily. Slowly, with teeth bared, drooling saliva the rat advanced. Zirak backed up while he desperately tried to determine what defense to use. He was too small to outrun or overpower the rat, but he knew he was a good deal cleverer.

Suddenly, like a flash of white heat, an image flooded his brain: Zirak pictured each of his siblings dead from the bite at the back of their neck. Just as if a fog had lifted and the trumpet of battle had sounded, Zirak clearly saw what he had to do. All his instincts were alert and in battle mode. He was ready. Zirak continued to slowly back away from the rat, all the while tilting his head a little to the left. He wanted to tempt the rat into striking the back of his head.

The rat saw the opening and thought, "How easy this battle will be!" Then the rat poised to make his move. He dashed around to bite Zirak's neck, but at the last instant Zirak used his super-quick reflexes to duck and turn, executing a maneuver so sudden that it was hardly visible to the human eye. From underneath the rat's jaws, Zirak rose with venomous fangs ready and pierced the rat's vulnerable neck. In an instant he injected the deadly venom.

The rat was stunned! He could not believe this young cobra had outwitted him. No cobra he ever saw had such quick reflexes. The poison was spreading fast, and the rat was almost paralyzed. He could not move, but he could still see and hear.

Zirak drew close and whispered into his drooping ear, "Your tasty treat was more than you bargained for, Garbage Rat. Let me thank you for the practice in how to dispose of neck-biters. I will use this lesson when I fight the mongoose Rikki-tikki-tavi."

Though powerless to speak, Garbage Rat understood that any mongoose had much more speed and agility than a simple rat. Also, he had frequently seen mongooses destroy cobras with several quick snaps of their sharp teeth. This thought gave Garbage Rat some consolation that Rikki-tikki could defeat Zirak. And yet, as he drew his last breath, he realized that despite his young age, Zirak had beaten him with cunning and lightning-fast reflexes. Zirak would be a formidable foe as an adult... even for a mongoose! Dejected by this final realization, Garbage Rat expired from the neurotoxins in the cobra venom that had shut down all his bodily functions.

The encounter with the rat convinced Zirak that it was time to move somewhere safer. The garbage dump had too many places were he could be ambushed, and the next time it happened, he might not react quickly enough. He considered the option of swimming back into the creek of flowing sewage, but he was not sure where it would take him. Instead, he followed a new path until it came to a long, brick wall surrounded by heavy brush. Searching for an exit, he crawled up a ladder of iron rungs set into the brick, and carefully avoided several sharp iron spikes that had pulled free from the bricks.

Near the top of the wall, Zirak found a hole in the bricks where he could look out. He peered through the hole and saw that he was near the middle of a street. Huge horned monsters pulling carts on wheels were moving back and forth, and Zirak had to duck for his life. He could not safely cross this street with all the moving monsters. When he looked closer, though, there were humans controlling the monsters. The humans were waving something over the monsters' heads that looked like a snake. Every time they jerked it back, Zirak heard a sharp crack, and the monsters jumped forward.

"What is going on here?" Zirak thought. He watched carefully for many minutes; his thoughtful study was rewarded when one of the monsters stopped, and several humans got out. "Tie up the oxen and put away this whip," one shouted as he rolled up the black, snakelike rope that he had used to control the oxen.

"Well, there you have it," thought Zirak. The horned monsters were oxen pulling carts, which the humans used to move their possessions. The snakelike rope was called a whip and seemed to be an effective weapon. He tried to duplicate this whip, and with a flick of his tail, almost caught a butterfly in mid-flight. Several tries later he actually tipped the butterfly wing. This success convinced Zirak that with practice, this new technique could be a valuable addition to his deadly fangs.

He was now looking at a bazaar or market where the humans came to trade foodstuffs and new articles like the discarded items he had seen at the garbage dump. A snake charmer was serenading one of his brother cobras that slowly rose from a basket. "Why doesn't he strike the puny human?" thought Zirak.

As he watched and wondered, he involuntarily started swaying to the music and slow hypnotic movement of the snake charmer. It seemed so soothing to just watch and listen with no thought of danger or future problems. Time seemed to stand still and Zirak felt the same warmth and comfort that his mother's loving hisses brought forth while he was still inside his eggshell. How pleasant it all seemed... How wonderful it would be, Zirak though, to simply let go of all his worries and curl up inside the charmer's basket.

For several moments, Zirak was under the charmer's spell, but he quickly shook his head and regained control of his senses. His respect, fear, admiration and wariness toward the humans increased significantly. They were clever, and he must respect their use of machines and tools if he was to have his revenge. However, he also knew instinctively that the humans feared his kind, as well they should, since one bite, however slight, would dispatch them to the god Brahma.

Zirak reluctantly returned to the edge of the creek and slithered into the moving debris leaving his fate up to Brahma and the whim of the current. The creek carried Zirak for many miles. New vistas and creatures appeared around every bend. Birds of every kind were flying overhead. Brilliantly colored parakeets, macaws, cockatoos and lorikeets plumed with every hue of the rainbow were everywhere in large flocks; sometimes there were so many that they momentarily blocked out the sun. Even the creek returned to life as new brooks brought clear fresh water. Frogs and beautiful pastel green lizards abounded, all of which helped to feed Zirak's voracious appetite from the exertion of the long swim. Finally the creek emptied into a large river, which was called Ganges by the humans.

It felt good to be away from the garbage dump and the sewage and to enter into a fresh, wondrous area with an enormous river of clean water. On the opposite side of the river Zirak saw a grassy bamboo area that he instinctively knew would be a safe haven. Cobras thrive in grassy bamboo areas because they provide shelter and food. Many small animals fatten up and feed on the bamboo plants. So Zirak would enjoy good hunting there. He rested on the bank basking in the warm sun for a while to build up his strength before swimming to the other side.

Cobras are excellent swimmers, but the river was wide, and there was no need to rush to the other side. Once fully refreshed, warmed and rested, Zirak contentedly began swimming toward the bamboo area. Zirak always planned ahead. He had carefully chosen a spot upstream where the river current and his own movement would land him exactly on the bamboo grove.

Many objects floated near him, carried by the lazy current. Uprooted water lilies, ferns, dead insects and a dead river terrapin were only some of the flotsam. There was also a variety of leaves and tree branches blown free by a storm further upstream.

Suddenly, Zirak's keen senses warned him of danger! A large log seemed to be floating toward him, but it was moving against the current and somehow looked alive. Instinctive visual memories from his ancestors flashed a subconscious warning, and Zirak knew instantly it was a crocodile. Zirak swam desperately toward the shore. The crocodile was a much faster swimmer, but it was fighting the current. Fortunately, Zirak had noticed the croc before it came too near. It was a close race, but Zirak managed to swim out of the river and slither onto the bank just before the crocodile's jaws snapped at his tail.

Zirak was exhausted from swimming for his life. He slid into the heavy grass. Varied flora and shrubs radiantly displayed themselves. Birds, insects and brilliant blue butterflies were everywhere. Around him were bamboo groves, heavy deciduous trees and thorn bushes, all of which provided excellent hiding places. He slid over a rocky outcrop and discovered an abandoned Bengal fox den – a small cave flanked by rocks and cut into the earth. This cave suited his needs perfectly. He entered the den and curled up into a ball with his head and fangs guarding the entrance.

Zirak fell asleep instantly but had repeated nightmares. Over and again in his dreams he saw Rikki-tikki destroying his family. It was terribly sad for him to revisit the carnage of the burrow. He woke several times that day, each time finding himself alone and still orphaned… and each time renewing his vow to avenge his family by returning to his birthplace and eliminating Rikki-tikki and the humans.

Night fell, and Zirak awoke refreshed but hungry. He left the den to hunt for food, with the cooler night air suiting him just fine. India's hot climate, even at night, coaxes many Indian cobras to hunt by starlight

— sometimes even entering homes looking for rats that usually raid the human food pantries. Hunting in human homes often results in a deadly encounter, either for the cobra or the humans who live there.

Fortunately, Zirak did not have this problem. No homes were yet built in his area. It was a paradise that humans had not yet ruined. Near the river, food was everywhere – frogs, lizards and small birds were easy prey. Zirak grew stronger and more skillful as a hunter with each passing day. It had been twelve months since his escape from the melon patch.

Zirak often spent his days on a rocky outcrop sunning his shiny, dark olive skin. He had just shed his old coat for the twelfth time. Zirak was growing so fast that he literally outgrew his skin monthly rather than the four to six times a year that most of his fellow snakes did. With every skin shedding, his color and markings grew more brilliant. The dorsal spectacle mark shined like gold on the back of his hood: this mark of the ventral yellow ocellus resembled a golden pair of eyeglasses tattooed on his back. He felt that it gave him the appearance of seeing in all directions.

Zirak admired his freshly molted body and was pleased to observe he was now over eight feet in length. Indeed, he was at least two feet longer than any other of his species, and did not expect to get much longer. His girth was also thick and heavy, as wide as a man's forearm. Plentiful food and superior genes had resulted in a dramatic growth. Most noticeable of all were his fangs — now over two inches long and as thick as one of the iron spikes he avoided when climbing the brick wall. Unlike the dull grey spikes, these fangs shone like ivory and were extremely sharp. He often enjoyed opening his mouth wide to admire their reflection in the small pool of water near his burrow. He also used the reflective pool to practice the flicking of his tail to produce a whip-like action. He had mastered the skill entirely and was able to stun frogs and even fast moving hummingbirds that approached close enough.

One night, hunting near the edge of his territory, he encountered a field rat almost twice as large as the Garbage Rat that had struck such fear during the first encounter. Oh, how different this meeting was! No longer did he seek to flee in panic; no longer did his heart beat fearfully. He stealthily closed in on the rat that was busily occupied eating a dead bird.

Not a leaf stirred to warn of Zirak's presence as he came nearer to the rat. When he was close enough, he raised himself to one-third of his height and closed the final distance in a flash. At the last moment the rat sensed Zirak, but it was too late. Zirak struck instantly and fiercely, his fangs sinking deeply into the rat's body. Zirak shook his head furiously, injecting much more venom than necessary. At that moment he was imagining that he had caught Rikki-tikki... His hatred and desire for revenge overtook his actions as he mercilessly shook the dying rat.

Zirak often thought about returning to the garden house. He still felt that he needed more time to grow wiser and stronger, but there was another, more pressing problem to solve first. The creek discharge he had escaped from was on the other side of the river.

Swimming would be no problem since all cobras are excellent swimmers. The problem was the crocodiles. Many times he had observed from his rocky vantage point how they captured all sorts of prey — ducks, deer, and even water buffalo. No animal could escape their combined menacing attack. How sly the crocodiles were, pretending to be logs floating in the water or merely hiding submerged near the shore. Their attacks were swift and deadly. With large jaws and rows of sharp teeth, they captured any animal that came too near. Small prey they swallowed whole; larger animals were torn apart by a pack of crocodiles acting in concert. Even though he sat on a warm outcrop, chills and shivers went through his body as he remembered his own close call.

Far away from his post, at the outskirts of his territory, Zirak saw movement. Using his superior eyesight, he observed that the humans crossed the river daily without danger. They used another of their machines called a boat. These humans were always thinking — dangerous foes to say the least, Zirak thought. But he, too, was capable of deliberate planning and observation. Zirak concluded from his own careful research that the humans were most vulnerable at night. Their eyesight grew poor as the sun set, while Zirak's seemed to improve. Many times in the dark of night he had crawled unseen, close to their campfires, and had watched them carefully to learn their secrets.

Then one night he happened upon a discovery so chilling that he was almost afraid to recall the memory. A rogue tiger had chanced upon the camp and had started to attack the cattle. One man jumped into the melee armed with nothing but an odd-shaped stick.

"What madness is this?" Zirak thought. The tiger turned from the cattle to devour the pitiful man. It roared loudly, shouting defiance. The tiger crouched low, ready to spring with jaws snapping and claws ripping. Using the strength of its powerful hind legs, it leaped ten feet into the air, hurtling toward the helpless man.

Then came the part that Zirak couldn't comprehend: the man pointed the odd-shaped stick at the tiger. Thunder, fire and lightning exploded from the stick! The tiger was dead instantly, even before it hit the ground. From his hiding place Zirak had learned another important lesson: never go near a human when they carry the "stick that explodes". Still trembling from the awful experience, Zirak returned to his den to rest.

Time passed swiftly and pleasantly for Zirak. He was now almost two years of age. He hunted at night and in the early morning, before the humans were about. All snakes become sluggish with cooler temperatures, but India's warm nights allowed him to remain active whenever he chose.

His favorite food was fresh rat, partly because he remembered his childhood encounter, but largely because one rat satisfied his hunger more than a dozen frogs or lizards. After swallowing the paralyzed rodent whole, he would go to his rocky plateau to sun himself, digest his meal, and watch over his territory. He constantly observed the flowing river, searching for a way to cross that would avoid the crocodiles. The crocodiles enjoyed sunning as much as Zirak, but despite their sleepy appearance, they were always ready to dash into the river to catch some unfortunate animal. Zirak pondered the problem and searched for a solution.

RIKKI-TIKKI, THE HONORED FAMILY PET

Meanwhile, back at the garden house, Rikki-tikki was the center of love and attention. Small pieces of sweet meat, bananas, eggs and a variety of foods were given to him daily. Teddy would feed him scraps from the family table; one meat called bacon Rikki-tikki especially liked. He was careful, though, to eat moderately and to stay trim because he realized that his quickness was what kept him from losing any battle with a snake.

To keep physically fit, he made numerous patrols of the house and veranda, checking the garden and stables in particular. Typical of his breed, Rikki-tikki was curious and energetic. Nothing escaped his attention. After his early morning inspection of the garden premises, he would dash about the house checking every nook and cranny. He would climb on the counters and table poking his tiny pink nose into everything.

Rikki-tikki wasn't just looking for snakes; he wanted to see everything all at once. Sometimes in his excitement, he would tip over a milk glass or fruit bowl, and Father would complain. Once he even broke one of Mother's favorite teacups. Mother never scolded Rikki-tikki, and she chided Father for being upset. She said Rikki-tikki was "just happy" to be with them, and after all, "Didn't he save the whole family?" Father just grumbled, but in a pleasant sort of way because he loved Rikki-tikki as much as anyone else and knew that the debt owed to him could never be repaid.

Night fell, and Rikki-tikki would hop on the bed to sleep next to Teddy. Mother would look in with a contented smile as she watched the two snuggle together, happily drifting off to sleep. She felt secure in the knowledge that Rikki-tikki was there to protect her family. Even though he was still a youngster, Rikki-tikki would awaken several times during the night and patrol the house. These night patrols were done quietly since Rikki had learned that even Mother couldn't keep Father from being angry if Rikki accidentally woke him at 3:00 am. Time passed pleasantly for Rikki-tikki and his family with no signs of any snakes, cobras or other intruders.

Then one day, Teddy's parents took him to the zoo. Naturally, Rikki-tikki went along, hidden in Teddy's coat pocket. What wondrous sights there were to see! Lions, Bengal tigers, elephants, parrots, peacocks, monkeys and many different animals — each kind lived in a separate habitat enclosure. Rikki-tikki could hardly remember all their names. He was timid at first until he realized the animals could not get across the barricades to hurt anyone. The lions roared but quickly got tired and rested in the sun, peering across the safety of the chasm. As soon as Rikki-tikki made that discovery, he boldly perched on Teddy's neck craning to see the next exhibit.

Monkeys, antelope, even a black jaguar, each animal in turn was marvelous for Teddy and Rikki-tikki to watch and discover. Teddy's parents smiled at both of them; parental pride and excitement shone from their faces as they watched their son and Rikki-tikki take in the wondrous sights for the first time. There was one moment of concern when they passed the serpent building, and Rikki-tikki's instincts caused him alarm. They quickly bypassed that exhibit, and about one hundred yards later, Rikki was back to his perky, inquisitive self.

Then something wonderful happened. The family came upon the

mongoose exhibit. It was a large open area, almost as large as a football field. There was an empty, steep concrete trench all around the exhibit and fencing in front to keep the people from falling into the trench. Imagine his surprise and delight when Rikki-tikki saw several dozen of his kind frolicking around a termite mound not more than twenty feet from the fence!

"Hello there! I'm Rikki-tikki-tavi," he chattered cheerfully.

"Hello," the entire pack chattered in unison. "Come, everyone, and see Rikki-tikki-tavi, the slayer of the cobras Nag and Nagaina and destroyer of their entire clutch of eggs."

"How could you know this?" Rikki asked.

"Everyone in the zoo has heard of your fierce battle with the cobras," they chattered excitedly. "Idok, the Indian grey hornbill told us," they shouted. "He heard the news when he passed your cottage. Darzee the tailorbird sang joyfully, proclaiming your victory, no longer fearing that Nag and Nagaina would eat his fledglings. Idok, a friend to the mongooses, often acts as sentry from his high perch to warn of danger from eagles or hawks. Sometimes after a journey to the outside of the compound, he returns with exciting news. All here in the zoo have heard how you saved Teddy and his parents from the wicked cobras. Idok said that you were truly brave and resourceful, especially considering you were only a mere youngster at the time of the attack."

From somewhere in the pack a small voice was heard, "And handsome, too." It was Norla, the young female, who finished her comment with a sigh. When Rikki-tikki heard Norla sigh, his pink nose turned red, and he felt a flush throughout his body. Their eyes met, and in that instant Rikki-tikki fell hopelessly in love. What a beautiful mongoose she was, grey shining fur, preened to perfection, with dark soulful eyes.

"He – he – hello," Rikki stammered. "What is your name?"

"Norla," she replied, her heart pounding so loud that everyone could hear.

The mongoose pack returned to their normal routine and let the love-struck couple continue flirting. Norla came to the edge of the trench while Rikki-tikki pushed his head through the fence opening to get as close as he could to her. They talked about silly things, the way young lovers often do, but each one thought the other was terribly interesting and eloquent.

Rikki-tikki tried to keep Teddy there all afternoon so he could continue talking and staring at Norla. Teddy and his parents could see how much Rikki-tikki wanted to stay, so they waited as long as they could until it was finally time to leave.

"I will be back to see you soon," Rikki-tikki promised.

"As soon as you can, I will be waiting anxiously," Norla chattered with her cute ears twitching. Then she sighed one last time as Rikki-tikki turned to leave.

Rikki-tikki was subdued on the return trip home, sad yet happy. Teddy tried to reassure him by stroking his fur and promising to return to the zoo very soon. He was overjoyed and nuzzled Teddy's neck to show his appreciation.

The family made several more trips to the zoo, and soon all the animals knew that Rikki-tikki and Norla were in love. George the Giraffe, because he was so tall, would be the first to see Rikki-tikki coming. Being mute like all giraffes, George would butt his head against the side of a metal shed to let all the animals, especially Norla, know that Rikki-tikki had arrived. The noise he produced could be heard throughout the zoo. It sounded like thunder or a big bass drum.

Norla would climb to the top of the termite mound and wait anxiously to see Rikki-tikki. They talked some, but it was hard for them to say what they felt in front of such a large audience. So most of their visits were spent giving each other a look or a glance that each knew meant a promise to be together. When it was time to leave, each of them sadly said farewell. Norla lay flat on the earth and put her head on her front paws and almost burst into tears. Rikki-tikki knew he had to do something soon.

Then one day Father came to the house with important news. His regiment was to be transferred to Calcutta for the summer to control a small uprising. They would be housed in small temporary quarters along with several other officers' families. They were required to close their house for the summer and bring only bare necessities because there would be very little room for each family. Teddy and his parents instantly looked at Rikki-tikki. There would certainly not be enough time or room for his energy and antics. Teddy began to cry, but mother quickly consoled him.

"Now, there must be some answer," she said. "We cannot leave him alone in the house, and we can't take him with us."

They all sat at the teak table thinking, even Rikki-tikki. Teddy was the first to come up with the obvious answer.

"He could stay at the zoo with his girlfriend Norla!" he shouted. "There he will be safe, cared for and happy." Everyone thought that was a terrific solution, especially Rikki-tikki who jumped on the top of the table, did a few back flips and gratefully nuzzled the whole family, each in turn. At last, he and Norla would get to spend some real time together.

RIKKI-TIKKI MOVES TO THE ZOO

Father arranged with the zoo director to let Rikki-tikki stay for the summer with the other mongooses while the family was in Calcutta. On the day they were leaving, everyone had mixed emotions. Mother, Father and Teddy all loved Rikki-tikki dearly, and he loved them equally. The saving consolation was that the separation would only be for a few months, and Rikki-tikki would get a chance to see Norla regularly. With that thought, they placed him at the glass door that led from inside the zoo to the outside termite mound and mongoose burrows. He gave each of them farewell nuzzles, and with an extra poke of his pink nose for Teddy, he bolted through the door to meet the troop and, of course, Norla.

As soon as he reached the termite mound, he was immediately stopped by Korna, the alpha-male and his wife Lida, the alpha-female. "What do you think you are doing here?" they both asked.

"Why, I am visiting for the summer while my master is away," Rikki-tikki replied innocently.

Now Rikki-tikki couldn't know the rules of living in a mongoose pack because he had been swept away from his mother before she had a chance to teach him. He had already broken the important rule that all mongooses know: they must show respect and subservience to the alpha-couple. This rule was absolute and if broken led to a fight to determine male dominance.

Rikki-tikki didn't know that a mongoose pack is controlled by the alpha-couple with the female providing a matriarchal rule and order and assigning various duties which included food gathering, sentry watch, house cleaning, child rearing and other chores necessary for successful communal living. Each one of the mongooses in the pack understood this law, and now all the mongooses, including Norla, waited on the side to see what would develop.

Rikki-tikki was disappointed by this turn of events. He really didn't want a contest with Korna. All he wanted was to spend some time with Norla. Moreover, if he did fight Korna and won, he would be expected to bond with the alpha-female Lida and help manage the pack. He was trying to sort out his options, when Korna started towards him in the weaving gait characteristic of a mongoose attack.

Growling and snapping with his head and back raised, Korna announced, "Fight or run Rikki-tikki. You have no other choice."

Rikki-tikki was not about to run, so he joined in the battle. What a flashing blur of adversaries they were. Dash, retreat, and counter-attack, they fought and weaved like two champion boxers whose moves were a blur to the average human eye. Indeed, their motions were almost too fast for even the average mongoose eye. But Lida and Norla both saw Rikki-tikki's jaws brush Korna's throat several times without dealing the death bite which Rikki-tikki certainly could have inflicted. Finally, after a full hour of fighting, they rolled together down a slope out of the pack's view.

"Three times I could have snapped your neck when my jaws passed your throat," Rikki-tikki said. "Call this contest a draw, and we can both leave with honor. I don't want to take over your role as leader; just let me be alone in peace with Norla. Hopefully, when my human family returns, Norla and I can both leave the compound together."

Korna understood and agreed in an instant, and they stumbled up the slope exhausted. When they were in sight of the pack, they nuzzled each other as a sign of friendship. Everything returned to normal immediately. The pack chattered happily and understood that Korna was still the leader, and that Rikki-tikki was his equal. Norla and Lida also agreed to equal status, each overjoyed that their respective mates were still alive! After the fight Norla took time to show Rikki-tikki around the compound and she cuddled him incessantly, relieved that he was not hurt. “Here is where we get our food and water,” she pointed to a small pond with pans of food all around.

“Where does it come from?” he asked.

"The zoo personnel bring some fresh food almost daily and keep the small pond filled with water. The rest of our food we find by hunting in the compound.”

“Don’t you ever feel like getting out of the compound and seeing the world?” Rikki-tikki asked.

"You are so silly!" she said. "We can leave anytime we choose. We have built burrows all over the compound, and more than one has a tunnel that leads outside. But who needs to leave a safe place, where food, water, and loving family exist?" Rikki-tikki thought about this for a moment and had to agree. The compound did offer quite a lot.

Norla spent the rest of the afternoon showing Rikki-tikki around and introducing him to her friends and family. She had a quiet strength and intelligence that manifested itself with every passing moment. That evening they went to a private burrow and spent the night snuggled together. They promised each other eternal allegiance and in the manner of mongooses became husband and wife.

ZIRAK FINDS A STRANGER IN HIS TERRITORY

Zirak was making the usual rounds of his territory when he came upon some slither marks in the soft mud. The tracks were large, but not as large as his. He immediately elevated his body, spreading his hood to see who dared to trespass on his grounds. Flicking the early morning air with his tongue, he turned a full three hundred sixty degrees to search out the invader.

A strong smell filled his senses. It was a pleasant smell and stirred in him a need to find the source. The source was a female cobra named Sarli who had been laying a scented track to attract a mate.

Sarli had been watching Zirak for many months. At first she thought his tracks were from another female cobra, since in the snake kingdom the females are always larger than the males. Imagine her shock and pleasant surprise to discover the tracks were of a male larger than she!

At three years of age, Sarli was ready to start a family of her own.

She was almost six feet long, but Zirak was two feet longer. Zirak was also three years of age and quite handsome with his shiny dark brown body and large hood covered with spectacled markings. It didn't take long for Zirak to follow the scented trail that led to Sarli. They met in a clearing just inside of a bamboo grove. Several lizards were surprised and bolted for their lives. The lizards could not have known that at that moment, neither cobra had any interest in them.

Shyly at first, the two cobras circled around each other. Zirak thought Sarli was beautiful, and he was overcome with her exotic aroma. All thoughts of aggression left him in a flash. Sarli giggled to herself when she saw his reaction. Her mother had told her how any male cobra would get dizzy and intoxicated from her pheromone scent and behave like a silly boisterous child.

"Why have you come here?" Zirak asked politely. He then rolled in her scent trail vigorously taking in its full aroma. Tongue-tied from the strong scent he stammered, "You, you really are... are pretty, and you smell wonderful."

Sarli turned her head sideways to stifle a laugh. Then, after gaining composure, she turned and gazed right into his eyes. "I have come here to meet you, of course." Zirak felt overwhelmed by the intensity of her stare, and cast his eyes downward, surprised by his own lack of aggression.

Sarli continued, "I need a husband, and never have I seen such a handsome strong brute as you. But perhaps you are a confirmed bachelor not interested in the responsibilities of a family." With this reply she gave a cute swish of her tail and pretended to leave the grove.

"Wait! Please stop!" Zirak cried, shaking himself from his almost trance-like euphoria. "I am the proud son of Nag and Nagaina. I would be happy to be your husband, and as my father before me, I vow to protect you as my wife for the rest of your life." Sarli nodded knowingly since she was aware that Indian cobras bonded for life. She turned back, and in the way of snakes they hugged each other by intertwining their bodies for several hours, promising each other lifetime loyalty.

Later that evening, they went on their first hunt together. What a pair they made! Swift and strong, any creature caught in their path was quickly disposed of. She would move through the heavy cover noisily to flush out the small animals and Zirak would strike unerringly as they came to the clearing. She could not believe his speed. Two lizards exited close to Zirak and each fled in opposite directions. He struck one to his left and then pivoted on a dime to catch the other all in a micro second. She beamed with pride and knew their offspring would never go hungry with such a provider.

Zirak and Sarli spent several idyllic months together, and all was well except for one thing. Almost every day Zirak told her of his vow of revenge against Rikki-tikki and his family. He told her of his plan to return to the humans' house and attack them all as soon as he solved the problem of crossing the river.

This plan frightened Sarli. She was afraid Zirak might be injured or killed and not return. She wanted to tell him the good news that they would soon have a family; but he was so angry when he recounted the story of how his parents and siblings were destroyed by Rikki-tikki that she decided to wait for a better moment.

The following day her worst fear was realized. Zirak burst into the den almost out of breath with excitement. "I finally found a safe way to cross the river without any danger from the crocodiles!" he exclaimed. "Come with me, I can't wait to show you."

RIKKI-TIKKI LIVES LIKE A MONGOOSE

Life with the mongoose pack was a barrel of fun. Every day there were new things to learn and enjoy. Most of the pack would wake early and nuzzle awake any late sleepyheads. Sometimes if he had patrolled late, as was his habit, Rikki-tikki would grumble good-naturedly, but then he would jump up and join the troop. Korna would lead the pack on a morning hunt as was his right and duty. However, he would allow Rikki-tikki to run at his side as an equal, and they soon became fast friends.

Rikki-tikki-tavi did indeed offer helpful suggestions to Korna, but always in a respectful way. Korna became like an older brother and taught Rikki-tikki-tavi all the rules of the pack. He also warned Rikki-tikki to be careful with cobras; he had seen his cousin die from a cobra bite.

"We are not immune to their poison," he warned. "The cobra can win the battle if we are distracted or caught unaware. You were lucky to overcome Nag and Nagaina... especially Nagaina when you dashed into her lair."

Rikki-tikki-tavi agreed and told Korna he knew it was only because Nagaina was preoccupied trying to protect her last egg that he had succeeded in defeating her. With that said, they both agreed that cobras were best fought with the entire pack rather than individually.

Every morning was primarily spent foraging for food. Some of the food was replaced regularly by the zoo personnel, who felt that active hunting kept the troop together by allowing them to use normal leadership and surroundings. Beetles, millipedes, crickets and sometimes even scorpions were found and devoured eagerly. Korna taught Rikki-tikki-tavi how to bite off the scorpion's stinger, rendering it harmless so that it could be eaten safely. Rikki-tikki-tavi liked scorpion meat a lot, but he still remembered that bacon tasted better.

After the group finished the morning foraging, numerous household chores were delegated by Lida. Some mongooses dug new burrows, others cleaned out the old burrows. Many females would help in the nursery with any baby mongooses. Others went on sentry duty to warn of any danger. Eagles and hawks could easily attack the open area from overhead. Idok the hornbill would help the sentries if he wasn't off fishing. In the event of an adversary's approach, the sentry would send out a shrill warning, and the mongooses would form a mob attack.

One day it was warm enough for the baby mongooses to be outside playing. Suddenly Idok and two sentries gave the warning cry. A large eagle was flying overhead. Quickly, the mongoose nurses shooed the babies back into the burrow. In a flash, the entire pack, led by Korna, clustered together. Rikki-tikki-tavi was amazed to see all of them with heads reared, snapping, growling and jumping together. This was a classic mob attack that the mongooses used to dissuade any predator from approaching the burrow. When the troop banned together as a mob, it succeeded in discouraging snakes, eagles and even large jackals. The eagle flew overhead for a short time, then left discouraged by the alert, united group.

The summer visit passed quickly, and suddenly it was time for Rikki-tikki-tavi to go home. Teddy and his parents came to the zoo to pick him up. Rikki-tikki-tavi ran to the top of the mound excitedly to get a better look. Teddy called out, "Meet us by the glass door."

Soon they were all at the door waiting, but Rikki-tikki-tavi would not come. He could not bear to leave Norla who was almost crying with the thought that they would soon be separated. Mother understood instantly as she looked into Norla's sad eyes. They talked to the zookeeper for a minute, and without much hesitation, all was settled. Norla and Rikki-tikki-tavi could leave together! What great excitement and joy coursed through the pack! All were happy for the couple, yet a little sad to see them leave. Each mongoose gave the couple farewell nuzzles. Korna practically choked with emotion as he told Rikki-tikki-tavi, "You are my new brother. Make sure you return often to see us."

Norla and Lida also promised to see each other often, and with soft goodbye chatter, they parted at the glass door. A carrying box was brought to transport the couple to the garden house. Norla felt it was too confining like a trap, but Rikki-tikki-tavi told her that as soon as they were home they would have the run of the garden. Sure enough, the minute they got home, Teddy turned them loose in the yard. Darzee the tailorbird and his wife both greeted them warmly. Chuchundra the muskrat hollered hello from where he was hiding under the rock. Several swallows and one parrot also chimed in to thank Rikki-tikki-tavi for making the garden safe.

Everyone was tired after the trip from the zoo and went to bed early. With Norla at his side, Rikki-tikki-tavi nuzzled close to Teddy. Mother looked in on the trio and smiled knowing no harm could come to Teddy while Rikki-tikki-tavi and Norla were protecting him.

ZIRAK SHOWS SARLI HIS RIVER CROSSING

Sarli followed Zirak for almost a half mile along the riverbank. They both were careful to stay low in the brush and grass to avoid being seen. They had traveled a long distance and were tired from the journey. As Sarli lay resting, she saw a large flat floor with a fence floating on the water.

"There it is!" said Zirak excitedly.

"What is it?" asked Sarli.

Zirak explained slowly because Sarli did not always understand how clever humans could be. "That is a machine the humans call a ferry. They use that rope to pull it back and forth across the river. People, animals, fruit and vegetables are all loaded on one side of the river and taken off on the other side. I have watched them for many days, and it is always the same until it gets too dark for them to see the opposite shore."

"What happens at night?" she asked fearfully.

"At night they tie up the ferry at shore and make their campfires and sing. One night I crawled under the ferry and discovered several spaces between the wooden barrels used to float the structure. When I crawl under the ferry into that space, no one can see me from above or below."

"How can you get in or out without being seen?" Sarli asked.

"Easily. I can get in after dark on this side as soon as they leave for their campfires. Once they reach the other side and unload, they usually have a meal and leave the ferry unattended. That will be my chance to exit unseen. Isn't it a great plan?" he asked proudly.

"No!" she shouted. "It is a horrible plan. It takes you away from me and our beautiful home, and it puts your life in danger. And for what? Revenge for the deaths of Nag and Nagaina? Certainly their own actions caused the confrontation with Rikki-tikki-tavi."

"How dare you talk about my parents that way!" he hissed loudly as he opened his hood and raised his body above hers.

"I dare because I love you, and I have kept quiet too long because I did not want to hurt you. My parents warned me and my siblings of living too close to humans when we were newly hatched. They had left the city because danger from the humans was everywhere. One of my brothers ignored the warning. He boasted that no one could hurt him. He was strong and smart, almost like you in many ways. He also found a way to reach the city. He returned several days later severely wounded from a spear and died shortly thereafter. My father was infuriated, but he stayed with our family instead of seeking revenge. Father warned us that death is the price of confronting humans, and my brother had made his own choice. We were all told that as long as we kept to our own area and avoided the city, we would be safe."

Zirak was confused and surprised by this lengthy outburst. Never before had Sarli spoken of her brother's death or her father's warning. He was uncertain how to reply, but then his anger overtook him, and he widened his eyes almost as much as his hood and spit out his answer. "I am not your brother! No cobra living or dead ever possessed half my abilities. I vowed to avenge my parents' death, and no one — not you, your father or the god Brahma — can change my mind!"

"Then do what you must," she shouted, "but don't expect me to be waiting for you when you return." Sadly she turned and slid off into the underbrush. He wanted to follow, but his pride prevented him. Confused by his own anger and overwhelmed by a myriad of emotions, he made his way slowly yet deliberately to the ferry.

ZIRAK MAKES HIS WAY TO THE OTHER SIDE

That night Zirak made his way successfully onto the ferry and into the space between the barrels. He slept fitfully because he missed Sarli and wondered if he should have gone after her. The ferry left as usual in the morning. No one suspected that Zirak was aboard except a pesky dog that kept barking at the floorboards. Luckily, Zirak was safely tucked away where the dog could not reach him, and after a short time, the barking stopped. The ferry finally reached shore where the humans tied it to the dock. After unloading all the cargo, the humans left.

Zirak waited several minutes to make certain everyone had gone. After listening intently and licking the air with his tongue, Zirak finally felt it was safe to come out from his hiding place. He slid into the underbrush and made his way toward the creek discharge. Moving slowly and carefully to avoid being seen, Zirak spent over an hour reaching the mouth of the creek. There was a small delay during which he noticed several crocodiles nearby waiting for some edible refuse. However, the creek continued away from the river, and he easily avoided any risk by entering the creek upstream, far away from the crocodiles' long jaws and sharp teeth.

Once immersed in the creek, Zirak had to swim upstream through the debris. The further he swam, the stronger was the stench and smell. The foul-smelling, moist air almost overpowered Zirak, who was now so accustomed to the sweet smell of his bamboo grove. Focusing intently, he managed to ignore the smell by savoring the revenge that soon would be his.

Several hours later, he reached the walkway where he had encountered his first rat. "How small it all seems now," he thought. The site was so much larger in his memory. There in a corner were the bones of the rat he had killed. Even the rat seemed smaller than he remembered. Tired and exhausted, he prepared to sleep in the large abandoned jar he had used as a youngster.

Suddenly he heard a noise from the creek, and he immediately became afraid that somehow one of the river crocodiles had followed him. He looked around desperately for a safe hiding place when he heard Sarli's voice.

“Zirak, help me… I am too tired to swim any further.”

Zirak plunged into the sewage and helped Sarli to the walkway. “How did you get here?” he asked.

"I followed you," she sobbed. “If I am going to be a widow, then it will be by your side rather than waiting for you never to return.”

“I am so sorry,” Zirak said. "I wanted to chase after you to apologize, but it was too late, I was confused… so I went to the ferry.”

"I know," she said. “I followed you and hid on the opposite side.”
“Then it was you I heard that night! I thought it was my imagination.”

Both were spent after the long swim, so they hid in the jar and went to sleep wrapped in a huddle to keep warm.

They woke early the next morning and continued the swim upstream through the creek. Soon the creek separated into several branches.

Zirak tried to remember which way he had come. After a few wrong turns, he finally found the brick wall and path that led to the garden where he had been born. When they arrived, he could not help but notice the look of dismay on Sarli's face.

"What is wrong?" he asked.

"This place, it is so small and ugly with none of the grasses and bamboo groves we have at home. No large rock area to sun ourselves... No river or pond filled with frogs to eat... It is so small, we could fit a hundred gardens this size in one part of the bamboo grove! How could anyone think to raise a family here?"

Zirak did not have an answer. As he looked out over the small garden, he began to doubt that his parents had chosen a proper place for all of them to live. He slipped silently through the small garden, and Sarli followed. They happened upon Torin, the aged tortoise, resting under a thorn bush. Torin was almost one hundred years old. He was not frightened of snakes, or of any other creatures. He lived in his large shell with thick armored plates that no bite could penetrate. He was wise and knew of the history of Zirak's parents. He looked at Zirak and calmly told him, "You must be the son of Nag and Nagaina."

"How do you know this?" Zirak asked.

"You have your mother's eyes," Torin replied.

"Tell me, oh wise one, did you know my parents? And how did they come to live in such a wretched small place?"

Torin was in a talkative mood, so he answered politely. "Yes, I knew your parents; and no, they did not willingly choose to live in such a small place, nor did they considerate it wretched. Once this whole area, as far as could be seen, was filled with bamboo groves, tall grasses, trees and a host of insects and wildlife."

"What happened?" Zirak asked.

"Man came and built houses, then a town, and finally this great city."

"What happened to all the animals and wildlife?"

"Most animals moved across the river where they could live in peace without interference from humans."

"What about my parents?"

"Your parents, especially your father, became stubborn and bitter and decided that no one would drive them from their home. Your mother pleaded to leave several times, but your father made the final decision that they would remain and fight for what they considered theirs. They were successful for a while since the house and garden was vacant; but then Teddy and his family moved in with Rikki-tikki-tavi… and you know the rest of the story."

Zirak looked at Sarli, and they both remembered her father's warning. "Could I have been wrong about returning all this time?" he thought.

Torin continued, "Your father's stubbornness was a dangerous mistake which, I fear, you may have inherited… otherwise, if you have found a home which makes this one seem 'wretched and small', what is the purpose of this visit? And why do you linger?"

The terrifying answer to Torin's question could be seen in Zirak's eyes. Torin perceived Zirak's vengeful mission and knew that all the wisdom of his years could not persuade Zirak to change his mind.

Just then Darzee the tailorbird caught sight of Zirak and Sarli. "Snakes, snakes!" he cried. "Two giant cobras are in the garden! Danger, danger! Everyone hide!"

All the birds and small creatures took flight or hid. Out on the terrace, Teddy's family wondered what all the commotion was about. Rikki-tikki-tavi and Norla knew from the warning exactly what had happened. They were poised and alert for action when Zirak and Sarli burst suddenly from the flowerbed onto the terrace. Ice-cold fear coursed through everyone's veins as Father warned the family not to move. He knew that any sudden movement could provoke a cobra strike. Even Rikki-tikki-tavi was filled with dread at the sight of Zirak! Never had he seen such a large Indian cobra! Zirak was longer than

Nagaina by more than two feet. The most worrisome part was Zirak's neck, almost as thick around as a man's arm. Rikki-tikki-tavi feared his jaws could barely open wide enough to get a tight grip on such a powerful and muscular neck.

Zirak hissed loudly when he saw Rikki-tikki-tavi, the slayer of his parents and siblings. He rose to almost three feet in height and hissed, "I am Zirak, son of Nag and Nagaina, the sole survivor of your massacre, and I am here to take my revenge!"

"How can this be?" Rikki-tikki exclaimed. "I destroyed the entire clutch of eggs that fateful day..."

"Or so you thought, Rikki-tikki-tavi, murderer of my family. The clutch was not complete. I was not with the others; my mother lovingly separated my egg from them, and spoke to me of her pride in my great size, telling me that I would bring honor to our family. I hatched several days before the others, and witnessed the slaughter you dealt my parents and siblings." This news almost overwhelmed Rikki-tikki, but he remembered Korna's warning and stayed fully alert.

Lucky it was, as his alertness was soon required. Zirak suddenly struck at Rikki with lightning speed and only missed his throat by a fraction of an inch. Sarli joined the attack and was followed immediately by Norla. All four stood in a circle ready to die for their loved one. "This is no good," said Zirak. "I did not come here to put my mate in danger. This battle is not hers to fight."

"I agree," chattered Rikki-tikki. "Let the females withdraw from this combat."

"So be it," said Zirak. "You and I, here and now, will fight to the death with no interference from anyone including the humans."

"One condition," said Rikki-tikki. "No matter what the outcome is, all the others must go free, unharmed."

Zirak thought quickly... Maybe killing Rikki-tikki would be sufficient revenge... And what was the harm in agreeing to his terms? If he changed his mind later, he could easily dispose of Norla and the humans after he vanquished Rikki-tikki. "Agreed," hissed Zirak as he nodded toward Sarli. “Leave us alone. The death of Rikki-tikki-tavi will be mine, and mine alone to savor! I will watch the buzzards feed on his dead corpse. Guard the humans and Rikki’s mate to prevent them from interfering.”

Obeying Zirak’s orders, Sarli left to confront the humans while Norla stood by, closely protecting Teddy.

THE FINAL BATTLE

There was another ominous click of the fangs with a near miss that struck fear into Rikki-tikki. It took all of his speed and agility to stay out of the reach of Zirak's jaws. Rikki realized at that moment that he could not defeat Zirak with speed alone; it was all he could do to just keep from being bitten. No ordinary mongoose could last more than a few minutes against such a formidable foe.

Rikki-tikki-tavi had exceptional speed and skill, but he had certainly met his match in Zirak. Rikki resorted to the instinctive mongoose attack of bob and weave. His movements resembled the jerky ballet of a skilled boxer. Feint and attack, bob and weave, the movements were hypnotic and reminded Zirak of the snake charmer. Every time he struck, Rikki-tikki had already weaved away, and Zirak's fangs snapped empty air.

Rikki-tikki had a careful plan. Zirak was using a lot of energy for the missed strikes. His bobbing and weaving defense did not require anywhere near as much energy; plus, mammals have much more endurance than snakes, even superior snakes like Zirak.

The one-sided battle continued for over twenty minutes with Rikki-tikki-tavi strictly on the defense, jumping, dodging and weaving to avoid the deadly fangs. After a while, however, he had tired Zirak to the point where the strikes were slower and less frequent. Rikki then launched his planned counter-attack.

In a flash Rikki's usual feint turned into a leap, and he managed to bite Zirak's wide neck. It was almost too wide for Rikki's jaws, and Zirak shook him free, catapulting Rikki-tikki into the stone wall and nearly breaking his ribs. But not before Rikki's teeth had drawn first blood! Rikki-tikki instantly realized that his strategy would succeed, but he needed to continue tiring Zirak with defense a while longer before he renewed the counter-attack.

Zirak could see the strategy of Rikki-tikki's plan and began to slow down the pace in order to gather his own strength. He also tried to think of a new plan to overcome the bobbing-weaving strategy that had stifled his progress. Rikki-Tikki saw the slowdown and attacked

Zirak on his backside and took several bites near his tail, jumping away quickly before Zirak could strike in return. Zirak was now bleeding from several deep bites and he needed an answer before this contest turned completely against him.

Zirak glanced around the terrace hoping for some inspiration. Then he saw it: a large ant mound near the edge. Carefully he maneuvered close to the mound. Rikki-tikki thought Zirak might be trying to escape, but that seemed unlikely. Maybe Zirak was more tired than he appeared. Then Zirak tilted his head a little and gave Rikki-tikki an opening. Just as Rikki began his leap, Zirak's tail snapped at the mound and flicked a host of army ants right into Rikki-tikki's eyes! Stunned by this unanticipated event, Rikki jumped backward and began to brush them away vigorously. Unfortunately, the damage had been done. His right eye had been bitten several times and was swelling up and beginning to close.

Serpentine movements with lightning speed
would Zirak succeed with this sinister deed?
Jaws of steel and saber-like fangs

Into the stone wall Rikki-tikki bangs

Dodge to the left, feint to the right

It appears there is no way he can win this fight!

Meanwhile, Sarli stood ground at the veranda protecting Zirak from any flanking attack. Once when Norla made a move to help Rikki-tikki-tavi, Sarli hissed a warning to stay out of the fight. "I do not agree with Zirak," she said,"but he is my mate, and I will kill you and all the humans here if you interfere."

Father made a slow move toward the "stick that fires lightning and death." Sarli remembered the story of the tiger and interposed quickly to position herself between the man and the fire-stick. Father retreated quickly.

"Why did you come here and risk death?" Norla asked Sarli.

"It was not by choice. I begged Zirak to stay on the other side of the river where it is beautiful and safe and the children I carry can grow up healthy and happy."

"You are with child?" Norla asked, suddenly feeling her fear and anger calmed by compassion.

"Yes," she replied, "my eggs are ready to be laid."

"I am also with child," Norla stated. A hush filled the veranda as both Zirak and Rikki-tikki-tavi realized for the first time that they were going to be fathers.

Upon hearing the news that Sarli was expecting, Zirak increased the intensity of his attack. With one eye almost closed, Rikki-tikki could not continue the attack. He kept retreating until finally, trapped and exhausted, he was forced into a corner. Both Zirak and Rikki-tikki knew that it was only a matter of minutes before he would administer the final bite.

Then suddenly, from the distance came a loud buzzing and chattering like a swarm of angry bees. Necks raised and teeth bared, the entire mob of over thirty mongooses arrived from the zoo led by Korna, Rikki's mongoose adopted brother. Swiftly the mob flanked and encircled Zirak and Sarli.

”How did you know I needed your help?” asked Rikki-tikki-tavi.

“Idok the hornbill heard Darzee’s warning and flew to the zoo with the news. We are your friends, your family, and our response was instant and came naturally to us. We quickly scurried through one of the tunnels under the fence to arrive here immediately. And not a minute too soon, I wager,” replied Korna.

The mongoose pack advanced relentlessly, and now Zirak and Sarli were hopelessly outnumbered. ”What treachery is this?” shouted Zirak. “We agreed no interference and to the death!”

“I made no such promise,” said Korna as he circled closer to Zirak.

“Nor did we!” echoed the mongoose family behind him. Zirak knew he had only seconds remaining before this fateful battle would end in a way he never planned.

“Stop!” cried Rikki. “I agreed to the terms and am bound by honor to accept the consequences. Do not attack, my friends. Leave this to me..."

"Honor!?" cried Norla, moving toward Rikki. "What code of honor did Zirak respect when he cheated and hurled red ants into your face? He was bleeding and exhausted; he knew his defeat was inevitable. He resorted to dirty tricks and the help of the ant creatures, to blind your eyes in order to win. He broke the promised oath first and deserves no mercy!"

Suddenly, amid the torrent of emotion, yelling and pandemonium, a stately figure appeared carrying a white flag. Ponderous in his gait, with wrinkles and scars of many seasons, Torin the Tortoise entered the center of the garden. His mere presence and calm, unaffected demeanor commanded everyone to stop fighting. As an audible hush fell upon the garden, Torin addressed the crowd.

"I have lived near this garden for almost one hundred years," he said. "I knew most of your parents, grandparents and great grandparents. Often, they came to me for advice and counsel. With joy and with a wisdom that overshadowed species and ages, I gladly helped whenever I could. Still, in 100 years, never have I seen this kind of fighting merely for revenge! We are animals, and it is our nature to fight only for food or to protect our families. The human is the only creature that kills commonly for revenge or jealousy."

Torin's wisdom and great age demanded respect, and everyone in the garden focused intently on his words.

"Rikki-tikki-tavi did nothing wrong by protecting his human family on that day so many years ago," Torin continued. "Neither in a sense did Nag and Nagaina by protecting their clutch of eggs; but they should have moved before the conflict occurred. I advised them often to move away from here, but they both were stubborn and refused to listen to reason.

"The humans caused the problem when they took our territory and cut down the trees and brush to make roads and houses. Before humans came, there was plenty of room for all of us to live here, on this very land, in nature's harmony. Once upon a time, as far as the eagle could see, this land was pristine and free from humans. The chance of cobra and mongoose meeting was remote, and usually each went about his own business without conflict."

Zirak listened impatiently, and wriggled in his own protest. "Maybe all that is true," he hissed with anger, "but Rikki-tikki-tavi killed my family, and I must have my revenge…!"

"So much like your father," replied Torin, lowering his eyes and shaking his head vigorously from side to side. "You are so blinded by your stubbornness that words of reason pass over your head as wind upon a melon leaf. I ask you then, oh wise Zirak so sure of his own destiny – what happens next? Will Korna and the pack then kill you and maybe Sarli? Perhaps later Sarli's father will come to avenge his daughter's death? And this new clutch of eggs, your offspring soon to be laid, could then awake to the same nightmare that you did. Will your revenge then be as sweet while your children suffer your pain, and inherit a legacy of revenge that you have created for them…?"

Zirak paused, speechless, as he pondered the unhatched eggs safe in Sarli's belly, soon to become his offspring. He reeled with instinctual, fatherly pain as he imagined his children being made orphans, as was he, and almost could not bear the prospect. He cast a protective glance in Sarli's direction as he pondered, seemingly for the first time, the great risk to which he had exposed her and their unborn children.

"It will never end!" continued Torin. "This killing is for no good reason!" Torin's voice bellowed and then quivered unusually with solid, emotional conviction. His eyes, usually gentle and slow, flickered with a pleading truth that pierced Zirak's own eyes like a spear. The truth was so obvious and so deep that Zirak had to look away. He could not refuse the logic of Torin's argument, which was so accurate that it had left Zirak speechless. He knew that he wanted to protect Sarli, but he still wasn't ready to give in.

A hush penetrated the crowd as each creature, different in his own way, began to look at the other with a new sense of reason and respect. "I propose the following solution," Torin continued, shaking his grey beard with authority. "Let Zirak and Sarli return in peace to their home on the other side of the river. In return they will vow to leave Rikki-tikki-tavi and his family alone. Let nature take its gentle course, and let peacefulness return to our behavior. Agreed?"

Both Sarli and Norla nodded their heads in immediate approval, and urged their husbands to do the same. Rikki-tikki-tavi soon agreed, but Zirak still had one more question for Torin. "What if the humans come to our home on the other side of the river and build a new city?"

"I will not lie to you," Torin replied. "What you suggest may one day come to pass. However, that will take a long time. You and your children will enjoy many pleasant days in your bamboo grove. Maybe by then the humans will find a way to build their cities and leave room for all of us to live.

"But if they do not," Torin added in an attempt to bring full closure to the situation, "we will ban together once again and move forward according to the harmony of our nature, rejecting the reckless killing of men... " All the animals nodded their heads in agreement. Norla rushed to Rikki's side, and Sarli quickly slithered to reach Zirak.

Torin turned majestically as the sunlight bounced off his brown body, turning it into a fiery copper hue. He carefully folded the white flag and told everyone to disperse. Each one and all together returned to their homes in happy anticipation of the days and years ahead.

THE END

March 12, 2008

www.ingramcontent.com/pod-product-compliance
Lightning Source LLC
Chambersburg PA
CBHW021621030826
48979CB00035B/1493/J
9780615222813